The Hero, The Sword, and The Dragons

The Chronicles of Dragon
Book 1

Craig Halloran

The Hero, The Sword, and the Dragons
The Chronicles of Dragon: Book 1
By Craig Halloran

Copyright © 2012 by Craig Halloran
First Edition

TWO-TEN BOOK PRESS
P.O. Box 4215, Charleston, WV 25364
ISBN eBook: 978-0-9884642-5-4
ISBN Paperback: 978-0-9884642-6-1

http://www.thedarkslayer.net

A cover Illustration by David Schmelling

Edited by Cherise Kelley

Publishers Note

The Hero, The Sword, and The Dragons

The Chronicles of Dragon: Book 1

Craig Halloran

Dedication

To my son, Nathaniel Conan. Words can never express how much you mean to me, but I wrote you a book anyway.

CHAPTER 1

I was running hard, pushing myself past human limits, to the only place I knew could help. Home. I already could tell that my wound was fatal, and with every step the loss of blood made me more woozy. Orcs were hot on my trail, at least a dozen, howling for my head. I was certain they would not stop; they were stubborn and stupid, slow as well, but I was smart and fast. I was a dragon, after all... in a very man-like sort of way. By appearance, I was a man: big, long-haired, and rangy—more than capable of whipping a few lousy dragon-poaching orcs, until they got the drop on me. So now I was running for my life, my dragon heart pounding in my chest like a galloping horse mile after mile until I had no choice but to come to a stop. I looked down at the crossbow bolts protruding from my side, through my back.

"Egad!" I exclaimed, checking the wounds. The blood had already stained a patch in my armor, and I knew it was still worse than it looked. Every breath I took was pain filled and biting. I knew I was bleeding inside, and I had to stop it or die. I pulled the lid from my canteen and drank, which did little to quench my thirst, but it brought some relief. I reached inside my satchel, my little bag of tricks, and fumbled for a vial.

Over the years, I've picked up a few useful things, like potions. Magic potions. They can do many things. Turn you invisible. Make you bigger. Smarter. Faster. Stronger. And even heal. In this particular case, it was a healing potion, in a vial as big as my index finger, which was pretty big, but it only looked to have about one drop left as I shook it before my eyes.

"Ugh,…" I moaned, the pain not getting any better, "I don't think this will do it." I looked down at my wounds and tried to decide: should I take out the wooden shafts first, or afterward? I'd been hurt before, plenty of times, but this festering wound was a tricky one.

"Just do what you always do, Dragon."

That's what I call myself, and I talk to myself a lot. My real name is much longer, difficult to pronounce and spell, but part of it is Nath. So, if a commoner ever asks, Nath Dragon is my name; saving dragons (and other things) is my game.

I tore a piece of bark from a tree, pinched it between my teeth, and bit down. Beads of sweat erupted from my forehead as I began pulling the first bolt through my skin. The good thing about them being crossbow bolts was they weren't as big as arrows, but they sure did pack a punch. I groaned, certain I was going to die as I ripped the rest of the shaft free.

I felt sick. My skin turned clammy, and the sound of the woodland crickets became loud and irritating. In the woods there are many dangers, and I wasn't anywhere close to being out of harm's way. Anything could pick up the trail of the wounded: overbearing bugbears, wily wood elves, pesky witches, dog-faced gnolls, transforming wolves, tricky sprites, were-shadows, or even worse … dragons. Yes, there are bad dragons, too, but it wasn't likely I'd run into two dragons in one day, or that a dragon would want to fool with me, for that matter. But they did, on occasion; I'd seen it for myself. The most beautiful and dangerous creatures in the world. The noblest and greediest, too.

"Do it, Dragon!" I was gritting my teeth on the tasteless bark once more. The pain was excruciating, each bloody inch I tugged free twice as painful as the last. *Don't black out.* A wave of wooziness assailed me as I got the last bolt free and slipped to my hands and knees, trembling like a leaf. I put the healing vial to my lips and watched that last pink drop slide down the tube and land on my tongue. Elation. Exasperation. It coursed through me, head to toe, mending every fiber, sealing every unnatural pore. The relief was astounding, but the healing incomplete. As quick as it started, it had stopped, but at least I wouldn't be dripping blood anymore. Spitting it, perhaps.

Clatch-Zip!

Clatch-Zip!

Two bolts ripped past my face and quavered in a nearby tree.

"Stupid bloody Orcs!"

I pushed myself to my feet with a groan and began sprinting through the woods, each step feeling like a punch in my stomach. I had to get home, find my father, and explain to him how I had gotten whipped by orcs, which never would have happened if I'd been allowed to kill them in the first place.

Zip! Zip! Zip!

My legs churned harder and harder as I began to outdistance my pursuers, cutting across the grassy plain, and the barrage of bolts began to subside. So on I ran, the sounds of the angry orcs fading away, leaving only the wind in my ears and the sharp throbbing pangs in my stomach. I just hoped I had enough strength left to return home.

Of course, my father probably wouldn't be too pleased by my return, either. I had his sword that I named Fang, a beautiful glimmering object of steel and magic woven together like its own living thing. Well, it wasn't given to me; I sort of borrowed it, and by then I was pretty sure my father would know it was missing. He wasn't the most understanding when it came to such things, either.

So I ran, through the shallow waters, over grassy gnolls, by shining cities whose towers almost reached the clouds, each long stride a hair shorter than the last, until I made it to just within my keen eye's shot of the Mountain of Doom and collapsed.

CHAPTER 2

As the sun rose, warming the chin hairs on my haggard face, the last thing I remembered was the blackness of the coming night. For all I knew, I'd been asleep for a day. I don't think a screaming ogre could have woken me. At the moment, everything felt fine. Then I moved.

"Ahg," I said. I wiped the morning drool from my mouth and spat out the tangy taste of my blood. I still had miles to go, and I wasn't so certain I could make it. Upright as I could be, I staggered forward. My stiff legs were no longer capable of churning after days of running off and on, but I knew I had to keep going, seek help, and not die.

Ahead was the Mountain of Doom, which isn't its real name, but a shorter name I'd given it because I never cared to take the time to say things properly. I swear, long names are given to things just so others will have something to talk about or just to give some little wretch yearning for knowledge something significant to do. I can spell it, backward as well as forward, but I'm not going to. Learning it once was more than enough already, and I see no need to repeat myself. It's just a word. But, the Mountain of Doom, my home, is beyond words. It's something you just have to see for yourself, and if you ever do, and you're wise, you'll gape in wide-eyed wonder, turn, and run away.

The base of the mountain is miles wide, maybe a league or two. I used to have to run around its base as a boy, every crevice treacherous, loosely footed of shale, and streams of lava hot enough to burn your leg to the bone in an instant. That area is called the marsh of sulfur. The peak's nose reaches into the sky, snow caps blending into those cloudy skies, such as it was that day, before disappearing. Steam. Smoke. Those gases billowing from cave mouths, some small, others large and even enormous, seemed to illustrate that the mountain was more than a clump of rock and clay, but a living and breathing part of the world itself.

I wiped the sweat from my brow and fought for secure footing over the shale as I made it two miles deeper into the rising heat. The heat didn't bother me; I was used to that, but it wrought damage on my glorious mane of recently mangled hair.

I stood straddling the crest of a ravine, where a small stream of lava was flowing below. The face on the mountain, a frightful grimace it seemed, some said was a coincidence or a design of arcane wizards that once took harbor there. Or it was a massive scarecrow created by dwarves that wanted to be left alone. It was, without question in my mind, the face of a dragon. A massive cave filled with rows of teeth could be seen, smoke rolling from its mouth. The eyes shimmered with fire, and the nose holes dripped lava. It would be hard to argue that it didn't look like a dragon, that it was just happenstance, an illusion, something the feeble minded shared to encourage fear to be spread by other feeble minds.

I sighed. It was pretty much the reason no one ever came here, very often, and lived. Mile after mile I trudged along in agony, deeper into the valley of living lava until I had nowhere else to go but up. I looked back, the green grasses and tall trees no longer within sight, the rising mist now hid my view of the gentler, softer world.

The base of the mountain was sheer, black rock, no smoke, nor stairs, nor solid footholds. Not smooth, but rough, and spanning hundreds of feet high. This was the part that kept the adventurers at bay: the curious, the daring, the foolish, the greedy that wanted the dragon's hoard, rumored to be large enough to fill every household in an entire kingdom or more. It was impossible to get in, but to get out, with loads of treasure, it would take at least a thousand of the stoutest men to do that. Unless of course you knew a secret way, which it so happens I did know.

A natural archway greeted me like an old friend as I fell onto my knees before it. No runes, no nothing, just a familiarity that I had from long ago. I began to speak to it, my raspy voice struggling to be clear, as my tongue was thick and swollen with fever. Word after word, minute after minute I chanted in a language more ancient than man, more difficult than women, more lengthy than a river. It took thirty minutes before I finished, and nothing happened.

"Open," I tried to shout, slamming my fists into the rock. My voice was gone now, withered away like the ashes of a burning log, my efforts spent in failure. *Noooooooo!* I collapsed, holding my belly, the taste of blood filling my mouth, my last flavor before dying.

The archway shook and quaked, angry. From the corner of my watery eye, I saw a sheet of rock lifting. *Thank goodness.* I lay there, in pain, misery, and suffering, eyeing the portal open to safety, but unable to move. How long, I did not know. The archway shuddered and buckled, and the doorway began to sink down, a mouth closing, lips soon to seal shut. *Move!* But I could not. It seemed my death was likely to come first.

CHAPTER 3

Something powerful grabbed my arm and started dragging me though the portal as the doorway closed shut like a clap of thunder. Gruff hands rolled me over and pushed on the bloody patch on my armor.

I screamed so loud my voice began to crack.

"See, yer alive," a strong voice said, less hearty, more grim "…for the moment. Now let's get you patched up, restored to full health, so your father can be guilt free before he kills ya."

"Thanks, Brenwar," I groaned, "you always know what to say to make me feel better."

"Har!" He reached down and grabbed both my hands. "Up you go!" He almost jerked my arms from the sockets as he ripped me up from the floor. I looked down at Brenwar, with a frown as big as his, glowering in pain. My dwarven friend was as big and stout as a sand-filled barrel, raven-bearded, and armored in heavy metals from his chin to his toes. You'd think he'd sound like a wagon load of scrap metal when he walked, but all I heard as I followed was the sound of well-oiled leather rubbing together. I followed him up a cavernous stairwell designed for monsters, not men, spiraling upward without end. I knew where I was, but wasn't certain where Brenwar was going.

"In here," he said, stopping at an opening I swore hadn't been there a moment ago and shoving me inside. "Wait." His booted feet stomped up the stairs, echoing, then fading away.

I was in an alcove where a lone torch hung, its orange light offering a warm illumination to the scenes of many dragon murals painted across all the walls. I gasped as one of the images of the painting came to life. A female dragon, tall as me, slender and batting her eyes, walked over, her tail tickling my chin. I knew she was a female because her belly scales were lighter than the others. Male dragons tend to be darker. But if you truly know dragons, as I do, the eyes were a dead giveaway. The females have lashes on their lids, nothing too pronounced, but noticeable all the same.

Her scales, copperish and pink, reflected the most beautiful colors, and her comely face offered a smile. In her hands was a vial, the same as the one I drank from days before, that she tilted to my lips. I gulped it down, fell onto a pillow big enough for a cow, and let the magical mending begin.

I burned, inside and out, with satisfaction. My weary bones were revitalized. My innards—dormant, agonized and bleeding—now regenerated. My vitality was back. My aching feet were no longer sore. I felt as strong as a horse as I tore off my armor, stretched out my mighty frame on the pillow, and shouted at the top of my lungs with glee.

I swear the lady dragon giggled before she pecked me on my head.

"Thank you," I said, combing my hair from my eyes. The dragoness was beautiful, her features soft behind her armor and razor sharp claws. After all, beautiful things have to defend themselves. I waved as I watched her disappear back into the mural among her kind, a queen defending in a glorious battle of dragons charging across the sun glazed sky.

"Ah!" I elated.

I fell back on the pillow, wanting to sleep, as my mind told me I needed rest, but my body was ready to go.

"A bath perhaps," I said to myself, getting up, grabbing my gear and sword.

A gruff voice disagreed. "You can have your bath later, Nat—"

I glared at Brenwar.

"Er, I mean, Dragon. Your father waits." The husky dwarf walked over and took Fang from my hands. "I'll take that."

I held my head in my hand. I could leave now, if I wanted. I was healed and all the better for it. My father, he wouldn't come after me. He never did. He threatened to chase me down, but usually just sent Brenwar instead, who was slow. A team of galloping horses wouldn't make him fast.

"So be it," I said in resignation. Up through the Mountain of Doom I followed, one heavy step at a time, the revitalized feeling in my organs replaced with a queasy feeling. My energy, one moment endless, was now gone. Oh, I was fine, my health fully operational, but that didn't do much good in the presence of an angry father who I had been reluctant to listen to for quite some time. When we stopped in front of a massive set of doors that stood almost five stories tall, Brenwar looked up at me with a hard look in his eyes and said, "I told him you needed bathed, but he insisted that you come now." He reached up and patted me on my lower back. "I'll see to it your bathed before the funeral. It's been an honor knowing you, Dragon." With that, Brenwar, my only true friend in the entire mountain, pushed the door open far enough for me to squeeze through, and like a fat rat out of a metal can, he scurried away.

And there I stood, at the threshold of all thresholds, looking back over my shoulder for escape, but finding none. If I had some dragon scales by now, things would probably be all right, but I didn't. With great hesitation and a trembling heart, I stepped inside.

CHAPTER 4

Imagine the throne rooms of the greatest kings in the world combined and all their wealth lying at their feet. That's nothing compared to my father's throne room, and those kings are nothing compared to my father. There he sat on his golden throne, treasure covering the floor as far as eye could see, glimmering and twinkling in the light of the lanterns. Like a man he sat, more than three stories tall, monstrous wings folded behind his back, dragon head resting in the palm of his clawed hand, eyes closed. There had never been a king that big.

I pushed the door closed with a loud wump, stirring the golden coins that slipped from their pile towards the floor. To my relief, my father, a heavy sleeper, did not stir, yet my heart pounded in my chest. I supposed that it should be pounding in my chest, but I had figured that feeling, that nervous feeling you get as you tread into the unknown, would fade away with age. It hadn't. I pushed the hair back from my eyes and proceeded forward.

My father, the largest living thing in the world so far as I knew, was scaled in red mostly, a brick red, with trims of gold along his armored belly, wings, and claws. His taloned toe alone was almost as big as me, and I was big, for a man anyway.

"Come closer," he said from the side of his mouth. The power of his voice sent tremors through the room, upsetting more piles of precious metals and jewels.

I kept going, taking my time, having no desire to begin the conversation but very eager to end it. I stopped a good fifty feet away, craning my neck upward, trying to find the first word to say. My tongue was thick in my mouth, and I thought of all the brave deeds I had done, but it all seemed so minute before my father.

He snorted the air, opened his dragon's maw, and said, "You smell dirty. Like an orc."

That bothered me. He always had to say something that bothered me.

"It's good to see you too, Father," I shouted back, my words barely a gerbil's compared to his. And I was loud, loud as an ogre when I wanted to be.

One eye popped open, brown like a man's, but flecked in gold and glaring. The other eye opened as well, the same as the other, its intent no less hostile than the first. My father leaned back on his throne, long powerful neck stretching between the massive marble pillars behind him, that held the ceiling. He was glorious and powerful; his mere presence began to charge my blood. I was proud to have a father like that, but I hadn't told him so in a long time.

"Ah … the fear in your sweat is gone already I see and replaced by your spiteful tongue," he said, moving very little, poised rather, pleasant, as if he was being served dinner. "Still, it is good to see you, Son, as always."

That part got to me a little, but only because I knew he meant it. The way he said it was the truth. Everything he said was true, I knew, whether I wanted to agree to it or not. My father, which is what I called him, because his real name would take the better part of the day to say, had a voice of a most peculiar quality. Powerful and beautiful like a crashing waterfall. Wise and deep with all the wisdom in the world combined. Soothing and uplifting. But my proud ears had gotten accustomed to it over the years.

"Yes, well, Father, it's good to see you, too. There's nothing quite like taking a long journey home. Scraping and clawing for your life, bleeding out your last drop," I laid it on thick, "gasping for your last breath, only to be saved at the last moment of life, healed, only to be jostled and dragged here without a moment's rest." I began pacing back and forth, hands on hips, throwing my neck back. "And you complain, of all things, that I have not had a bath."

Ever seen a dragon smile, one with a mouthful of teeth as long as you? That's what I was seeing now, and it bothered me.

"Well, you know how I feel about those foul creatures, and I was excited to see you, smelling like orc's blood or not, and it's been so long, several weeks at least," my father said.

Now my father was being ridiculous. Dragons are never in a hurry to do anything. It takes them a minute just to blink. They aren't slow, by any means or measure, no matter how big they are, but they take their good time doing anything. Hours are minutes to them, if even that long.

I plopped down on a huge stack of gemstones, inspecting a few before tossing them away.

"Father, it's been almost a decade," I said, agitated. "Have you even moved since the last time I was here?"

"Certainly, Son, I've moved quite a bit since you've been here."

"I see." He never moved, except when it was time to feed, which wasn't very often. He hadn't moved since I was a boy, either. "Father, what would you know of me?" I had to push things, be impolite; it was the only way to make this conversation go quicker.

"I see things as well, Nath …"

"No don't!" I yelled, but it was too late. He began pronouncing my full name, which is as long as a river, syllable after syllable, ancient, poetic and powerful. I listened; minute after minute, mesmerized, my aggravation beginning to subside. My name was a beautiful thing: prosperous and invigorating.

"… nan." He finished, over an hour later. "Have you gained any scales?"

There it was. The dreaded question about my scales. Here I was, a son of the greatest dragon, but without a single scale. Despite all the right I had done, it seemed I'd done my own fair share of wrong as well.

"No!"

My father snorted. I saw a look of disappointment in his eyes, and I felt disappointed as well. I'd failed. Despite all my great deeds in the lands of Nalzambor, I was not living up to expectations.

He sighed, and it seemed such a terrible thing.

"How long, Son?"

I kicked at the piles of treasure.

"Two hundred years."

Like a man, my father reached up and grabbed his skull with his four fingered hands. I knew what was coming next.

"Son, the first hundred years of your life were the most wonderful of mine. You did everything I said. You listened. You learned. You grew. And when you became old enough, I let you choose. Stay in the mountain and continue to grow, or risk losing everything you are just to see the rest of the world." He shook his head. "I never should have given you that choice."

"I wanted to see things for myself. It was my right. You told me I needed to understand the world of men," I argued.

"Yes, I did. But I told you not to get too close. Don't get caught up in their ways. You are not one of them. You are one of us."

"How can I be sure? I still look like a man. I talk like a man."

He stopped me, head leering over at me, his eyes showing a glimmer of the infernos within.

"True, Son, but I warned you not to *act* like a man. I showed you what dragons do, how they act, how they respond."

I rose to my feet and resumed my pacing through the hoard, coins jingling beneath my feet.

"Maybe I don't want to devour herds of sheep and goats like a beast. I like my food cooked and making use of knives and forks. It's civilized. Unlike the dragons that rampage the flocks."

Father said, "The herds are for feeding, man and dragon alike. Forgive me for forgetting to use my knife." He waggled a talon at me. "If you had your scales, you'd understand, Son. You are meant to be a good dragon, the same as me."

I wanted to please my father. I really did. But, as the years passed and the hairs on my skin became more coarse, I had an aching doubt that I was ever going to become a dragon. There were many things that I could do that men could not. Living long was one of them, but I never felt sure.

"Father, how can I know that I am a dragon? If I was a dragon, certainly I'd have scales by now. The others do."

"Son, you are not like the others. You are like me. As I've explained, there are dragons like the rest, and there are dragons like us. I am the keeper of this world, a protector of men as well as the dragons. But I won't live forever, and who will protect them when I'm gone? It has to be you."

Me. Yes, I knew it was supposed to be me. Deep down in my heart, I knew it was true. But one would think I'd have a sister or brother to share the responsibility. I continued to pout.

"What about my mother? Will you ever reveal her to me?"

"Oh, stop. You were hatched from an egg."

"I was not hatched from an egg like a goose!" I yelled. It infuriated me, him saying that. I knew I had a mother, and I suspected she was mortal, but my father, truthful and wise, had been holding something back all along. And it infuriated me that I did not know.

"More like a little crocodile," he said, joking. "You had scales when you were born, we... er, I was so proud. But after a few years, they fell away." His voice saddened. "And that's when I knew."

He had slipped! There was indeed a mother; I was certain of it. But, I could not remember her face or anything of her at all. Was she a dragon or a mortal?

"Knew what?" I asked, even though I had already heard the answer before.

His voice was heavy as he said, "That you would be the child that replaced me. That the responsibility was yours, whether you liked it or not. As I did not have a choice, Son, neither have you. There is only one great dragon in the world, and if it isn't me, it must be you. Without us, the world is doomed."

That was it: the ship's anchor strapped onto my back. The burden of an impossible responsibility that weighed me down to my knees. *I didn't ask for this.*

CHAPTER 5

The more he kept talking, the smaller I felt. It was a big part of the reason that I didn't come home to visit too much. He told me about the Dragon Wars, where one brood of dragons battled another for the sake of mankind. Every race: man, elf, dwarf, gnolls, orcs, and ogres had been in danger those days, but the dragons, the good ones like my father, won out. It all happened long before I came, and it was impossible to believe that there had been such devastation. Mankind, all of the races that is, had been on the border of extinction. My father had sacrificed everything to prevent that, and he had the scars and missing scales to prove it. Still, it was all hard to believe, that life on Nalzambor had been so cold and hopeless.

I stretched on a sofa, as soft and exquisite as one could be, and listened again. There must have been something I was missing. Why didn't I have my scales? And yet again, he told me why he thought I didn't.

"For every life you take, you must save another, or more. It does not matter if they are good or evil, who can really tell? There is good in everything, evil as well …."

I knew better: orcs were evil. Gnolls, orcs, and bugbears, too. And renegade dragons, remnants of the Dragon Wars, were, too. It never made any sense to me to let them live.

He knew what I was thinking. "It's not just the orcs, Son. Men and elves can be just as bad. Have you not seen how they treat people? Would you treat your people like that? Outrageous."

It made sense. I'd spent so much time among them that I rarely noticed anymore. Some of their kind, men liked, and some they didn't like. They would feud and war with one another. Brag and boast about their riches, their kingdoms and princesses. I just laughed at them. They hadn't seen anything like I had, so their commentary was quite meaningless to me, but the company was very entertaining.

"My father was the same as me and you. He made this throne, but this treasure was here long before he came, even his father before him. And like us, they were born dragons that turned to men. You are not like your brothers and sisters, nor was I. They care little for the world of mankind, but it's important that we do. Men and dragons need one another. It's how life is."

I never really understood why dragons needed men, except to make treasure, which was still one of those things I enjoyed searching for in my journeys. I met many great men, elves, and dwarves, but I never saw any reason why we needed them. They tended sheep and cattle. Made objects that I assumed dragons were too big to craft. That was another thing. I never saw a dragon build anything.

"When I was your age, I was a bigger man, stronger, faster than the others. Our dragon hearts account for that. Like a horse's times two. I was cocky, too, for a while. I befriended the dwarves and learned about black smithing and forged the sword you've become so fond of over the years."

I jumped to my feet.

"You made Fang?"

"Indeed."

"But, if you weren't supposed to kill anybody, then why did you make the sword?"

"Because it's a symbol of truth, hope and strength. The men respected a man that swung a blade. And I never said you couldn't kill, just that it's only a last resort. But again, take a life, safe a life or more."

"How many did you kill?"

"Enough to remember, each and every one. Seeing life diminishing in a dying creature's eyes is a sad thing, indeed. We are here to save lives, not take them."

I thought about that.

"But don't we save lives when we take the lives of those endangering others?"

"How can you know for sure? At what cost, Son? Men will always fight and feud, whether we help them or not. They'll listen for a while, then wage war with one another. In all of your heroics, how much have you really changed?"

It was true. Battles were won and lost. Good men died, and bad ones lived. Evil withered in the dirt only to rise again into a strong and mighty tower. There was nothing that held it back for long. Not war. Not power. Not peace. This was the part that gave me a headache. Holding back against evil, the despicable beast.

"Save the ones you can, Son. Expect no rewards or thank-you's, and move on, which I don't think you are very eager to do."

I liked being with people, but they aged quickly, and sooner or later I would always have to move on. It was hard to watch them fight so hard for a life that wasn't long lasting. And maybe that was what I liked most about men. Every day mattered to them. Each one was new, never the same, filled with new adventures over every horizon. Men, good and bad, knew how to live.

I let out a long sigh. I still had no idea how to get my scales.

"I can see in your eyes that you are frustrated, Nath—"

"NO! Don't say it again!" I held my hands up.

"Sorry, Son. You should stay among your brothers and sisters awhile. I'd enjoy your company. Maybe my guidance will sink in."

He was talking another hundred years at least.

"No," I stammered, a good bit angry at myself, "I want to earn my scales. I want to be a dragon!"

My father leaned back, dragon claws cusping his knees, and said, "Take the sword. The one you borrowed. It was going to be a gift anyway, but you slipped out of here like a halfling rogue before I could gift it to you. Take Brenwar," my father's tone darkened, and so did his smoldering eyes, "and do not return this time without your scales."

"What? I can't come back?"

An impatient tone took over his voice like a dam about to break.

"NO! Take with you that which you need. You've earned that much at least, but do not return without your scales."

I shouted back. "Earned it for what?"

"Saving our kin. The dragons. Like I've told you to. Focus on the dragons. The little green one, Ezabel, was quite grateful for your intrusion. She sends her best. And she's not the only one."

"Really?" I said, surprised.

"Son, have I ever lied?"

"No," I said.

"Or been wrong?"

I remained silent. I wasn't ready yet to admit that, so I shrugged.

My father shook his neck, a column of red armor over pure muscle. Then he said, "I don't just sit here as you think and leave every once in a while to gorge myself on cattle. I do many things you aren't aware of. I see things that you cannot."

That was new, but I wasn't so sure I believed it. If he ever did pop out of the mountain, I was certain the entire world would know, each and every one would be screaming like the world was on fire. I know that I would be if I wasn't his son. Then I realized he'd gotten me off track.

"Am I really banished as you say?" I asked, unable to disguise my worry.

"Yes," he said, his voice stern. "It's time you decided. Do you want to be a dragon or a man? Which is more important to you, Son?"

It was a hard question to answer, and it shouldn't have been. Among the dragons, I wasn't so special, but among the people I stood out. The women, smelling like blossoming rosebuds, running their delicate fingers in my hair, whispering words in my ear that would make a bugbear blush. I liked it.

And the elves, when you came across them, were so pure and delicate in beauty. Their mannerisms were quaint, direct, their cores as strong as deep tree roots. A bit arrogant though, and I'd be lying if I said I didn't enjoy humbling them from time to time.

The dwarves, brash and bold, like my dearest friend Brenwar, were the fiercest fighters and stubbornest competitors of all. Hardy, grim, and a little mirthful, I found nothing but comfort among their kind.

"Ahem." My father interrupted my thoughts. "Do you really have to think about it so much? By now the choice should be clear!"

I waved my hands up in front of me, saying, "Oh, no-no-no father. It's dragons. I want to be with the dragons. It's just that I find myself feeling so sorry for the others." I lied to some small degree. I also wasn't so sure I wanted to sit where he sat forever, even with all the treasures of the world at my feet. There had to be more to what he did.

Father lowered his head all the way down to the floor, his face a dozen feet from mine, hitting me with a snort of hot air. I felt like an insect when he said, "I've been in your shoes and walked the same path, and I know what you are thinking. You think like a man. It's time to grow up and think like a dragon. Now, with all my heart and wisdom, it is time for me to go. Take care, Son."

He reared up, went around the throne, and melded into an enormous mural of himself that was painted brilliantly on the wall. All of a sudden I felt alone. His presence, for the first time in my life, seemed gone. It was clear that he was serious about my scales, and I'd better be getting serious as well.

I spent the next few hours shuffling through the piles, loading a sack with anything I thought might help me, knowing full well it was up to me, no matter how many tricks I had in my pack. I departed, taking one last long look back at the mural of my father and wishing that I was on the other side of the grand painting as well. Brenwar awaited me, leaning against a wall, arms folded over his barrel chest, bushy black brows raised with alarm.

"You live!" he said, more in a grumble, but a surprised one.

"Ha! You didn't really think he'd kill me, did you?"

"I would've."

"For what?" I demanded.

"Brenwar slammed my scabbarded sword into my chest.

"For stealing."

"Borrowing," I said, correcting him. "Besides, it was mine to take anyway."

"I know."

"You did?" I said, surprised. "But how di—"

"Just keep walking, Chatter Box. I'm ready to go. I feel so blasted small in this place. And there's no ale or dwarves…"

Brenwar kept going on, but I couldn't listen. My mind was too busy wondering if this would be my last time at home or not. My scales! I had my doubts I could do it, but determined I was, and a good bit deflated, too. How could I ever be a great dragon like my father? I didn't even have one scale.

CHAPTER 6

Brenwar's stout legs were too slow to keep up with my long legged pace, so we rode on horseback. Otherwise, he'd complain the entire way. I wasn't usually in such a hurry, so I normally preferred to walk, but I felt a degree of haste these days. Northward we went, towards the five great cities.

The Human city of Quintuklen was filled with magnificent castles and shining towers that overlooked vast rich and reaching farmlands.

The dwarven city of Morgdon was a mass of stone blocks and metal works, like a dwarven made mountain, grim and impenetrable.

The Elven city, Elomelorrahahn, which I just called Elome, the most majestic of all, was hidden in the fog and forests.

The Free City, Narnum, hosted all the races, at least all those not so monstrous, damaging or tormented. It was a trade city, where all the merchants from all the races came to do business, and I found it the most exciting of them all.

The most dreaded, not so vast, nor appealing, was Thraagramoor, or just Thraag, grim as a mudslide, crumb poor, and run by the orcs, ogres, and goblin sorts.

"Well," Brenwar said, "which way will it be?"

The Mountain of Doom lay in the south, leagues and days from the others. The cities were each two weeks' ride from the other. They formed a rough circle, with Narnum, the Free City, hosting the middle. Everything in between was unprotected and dangerous land.

"Free City, as if you didn't know," I said, hoisting my canteen to my lips.

"I thought we were to be rescuing dragons and such? There'll be no dragons in that city."

"Ah, but is there not talk of dragons wherever we go?" I was grinning.

"I say we go to Morgdon first, then. My kin will be happy to see you again." He stroked his beard. "Not so much as me, but they'll be glad."

Visiting with dwarves was almost as bad as visiting with dragons, except the dwarves were always working, drinking, smoking or frowning. Their voices were gruff, their conversations short, but they also took time to host their guests. They liked to talk about the things they built and the battles they fought in—with vivid detail. But if you'd heard one dwarf story, you'd heard them all. I was polite when I said, "How about on the way back then, Brenwar?"

He grunted, kicked his short little legs into the ribs of his horse, and charged forward. "To Narnum it is then, Nath! But by my beard, they'd better not have run out of dwarven ale, else I'll drag you back to Morgdon by your ears!"

I couldn't help but smile as he spurred his mount, the hot air of the sun billowing in my recently chopped hair thanks to the dreaded orcs. It would grow back before we made it to Narnum City, where I could find an elven barber to refine it with a dash of magic here and there.

We traveled dusk to dawn, over the plains, through the woodlands, over some mountains, through some small lake towns, and well past the ruins. All the way we chatted with caravans and merchant trains. It was spring, and farmers, miners, and merchants were moving along the dusty and cobblestoned roads, taking their wares to every city in the north.

As usual, I heard the same rumors of war, for there were battles and skirmishes everywhere. There were soldiers from many races, all eager to lay down their lives to make money for their families. Brave men we met, and I admired them all. Of course, there were others, too, up to no good. Some spoiled and bold and others as crooked as a busted dog's tail. But, I didn't chat too long. I had heard it all before. I'd fought in wars, myself.

Nearing the end of the tenth day, my hips were sore from all the hard riding, and words couldn't describe my elation when I saw the tiniest tip of a spire in the middle of Narnum City.

"Brenwar! We're almost there. Two hours' ride at most, wouldn't you say?"

"Aye, I can't see it, but I know the road as well as you. I knew when we were five hours away three hours ago." He snorted. "I knew we were a day away a day ago. I see no reason for celebration. It's not like we haven't been here before."

"Ah, it's just better to actually see it. Having the goal in sight. Can't you ever get excited about anything?"

"I'll be excited when I have a barrel of ale under my bones and a full tankard as big as my head. It looks the same as it always has: not dwarven."

Well, I was happy. The past few months I'd been outside the cities, tracking down dragon poachers and hunters. Life wasn't all fun and games for me, despite all my advantages, but when I went to the city, I made the most of it. And anyway, a place like Narnum, a mix of everything in the world, was where I went to find the ones who tried to hunt dragons.

This city in particular was different from the rest. A mix of everyone tried to thrive here, and for the most part it worked out. All of the races, good and bad, had a say in Narnum, which for lack of a better word was nothing more than a giant market place ruled by many dukes and earls that feuded with one another most of the time, paying little attention to the troubles of the people if they were not their own. There was never enough for most of them, and what they gained, they quickly lost. At least that's how I'd seen it over the past two hundred years.

A tower rose over three hundred feet tall, like an ivory tusk had burst from the ground. It was a beautiful thing. Massive windows adorned its circular walls where an outward staircase spiraled upward like a green vine. I could see tiny bodies moving and peering through the bay windows. I dreamed about the day I'd be able to fly around that tower, wings spread wide, soaring through the air. But for now I was a ground pounder, same as the dwarves and men.

The closer we got, the more people we saw: dozens becoming hundreds, hundreds becoming thousands as we approached the only great city that had no walls. A river flowed through the city, east to west. I could see the tall buildings, some reaching over a dozen stories tall, but most were not so tall at all. There were guardsmen and garrisons all along the way. The protection of the city was well paid for. The citizens, hard workers, liked it that way, and I didn't fault them. I'd want my efforts protected as well.

The roads were paved with cobblestones and brick. The markets thrived with activity as we trotted deeper into the city. A half-elven auctioneer worked the stage in the marketplace, selling pieces of jewelry to a crowd of excited onlookers. He was dashing, not as dashing as me, but his lips were as fast as a hummingbird's wings. Banners marking the neighborhoods fluttered in the air. Children played in the fountains, and some begged for coins. Women aplenty hung from the windows, whistling at me, to Brenwar's chagrin.

"Quit ta' flirting' will you! Let's find a tavern, eat, drink and make grumpy!" He was hollering at me.

One buxom gal was yelling my way, "Handsome warrior, will you come and stay with me tonight? I've the softest lips and pillows in all of Narnum."

"I can see that," I said, momentarily mesmerized.

The women kept calling to me, one compliment following the other.

"No, my pillows are softer."

"You are so gorgeous, and look at those broad shoulders! I will massage them all night."

"Your handsome eyes, are they your mother's or father's? I've never seen gold in a man's eyes, not even an elf's. So splendid and superb," a comely gal with long lashes noted, posturing from her window.

I stood and gaped at all of the wonderful things coming from their painted lips. I couldn't help myself.

Smack!

Brenwar jostled me hard in my side.

"Come on, Nath Dragon!"

I didn't budge … spellbound. Flattery was a weakness of mine, something my father had warned me about, but it didn't seem to ever sink in. I didn't want to fight what they were saying and saw no reason to, either.

"In a minute," I shrugged. "As you were saying, Ladies."

They all laughed and giggled as Brenwar took my horse by the reigns and dragged me away.

"Fool!" he grumbled. "You'll never learn, will you?"

"I hope not," I said, waving at the ladies, whose attentions faded from me and coated the next traveler with their wares and pleasantries. I frowned.

"Watcha frowning fer? You'd think you'd learn by now." He thumped his bearded chest with his fist. "Next time, I'll lead us in. You always go the same way. You're as drawn to those sirens as an orc is to stink."

"Am not!"

Through the city I went, my passions subdued, the sun dipping over the horizon. I led us into a less traveled part of the down, through some alleys and well off the commoner's path.

"Let's try this one," I said, pointing at a tavern, dark and dangerous, three stories tall, constructed of timber, and roofed in red clay tile. It gave me a shivering feeling. "There's plenty of trouble to find in there." So in I went, oblivious to the stranger's eyes that followed me from the road.

CHAPTER 7

There was music, hollering, and tale telling inside, and I liked that. Mostly men, of a questionable pedigree, long gazes and hard faces. The smell of roasted pheasant filled the air, and I was ready to eat. Brenwar pushed his way past me and saddled up to the bar.

"Ye got dwarven ale?" He asked a tall man, bald and wearing a black apron.

I took a seat alongside him, paying no attention to the stares glaring on my back. This city was used to travelers of all sorts coming and going all times of the night, but this place was one of those that kept close to their own.

"The same for me and two full pheasants, not charred, either." The two coins that I plunked on the table widened the barkeep's restless eyes. "And your undivided attention when I ask."

The barkeep slipped away, a small woman appearing moments later with two tankards of frothing ale as big as her head. Brenwar gulped his down in several large swallows, let out a tremendous belch, and looked at me.

"You can have mine," I said, turning my attention away from the bar and towards all the people inside.

Two men, one a bald giant, another part orc, each laden in muscle, arm wrestled over the wiles of a dainty girl with a look of trouble in her eye. A coarse group of men and women sat at a long table near the stone fireplace in the back, the adventuring sort, somewhat like me, some of them casting nervous glances over their shoulders.

An elven man wearing light purple garb and long pale green hair sulked in the corner and played a black lute of many strings for a small group of swooning women. His music was wonderful and strong. All in all, the tavern, a roomy little hole, was nothing compared to so many other taverns that tended to be much larger and more occupied. Still, it offered what I'd been looking for: trouble.

Three orcs sat in the back, beady eyes glancing my way and back. Another man, long and gaunt, sat huddled in the corner, fingering a blade, his tongue licking his lips as he gazed at me like some kind of meal.

At one end of the bar was a fair haired woman, a long sword strapped on her full hips, her tongue as coarse as the hulking man she accompanied, the one who had sneered at me earlier. I wasn't so sure they presented the kind of trouble I was looking for, but they were trouble. The kind that conspire and thieve. Rob grave yards, fight fiends and ghouls for gold. Kidnap women, sell children, and don't look back on their deeds with regret. Of course, my father would tell me not to be so judgmental, but I could detect evil, and it hung as heavy as a wet blanket in here. But did they trifle with dragons? That was what I was here to find out.

Brenwar's elbow rocked me in the ribs.

"Time to eat, " he said.

Two steaming hot pheasants greeted my senses with a delightful aroma. One thing you could say about these run down taverns of disreputable ilk: they tended to have tasty food. My stomach rumbled, and my mouth watered. I hadn't realized how hungry I was until I started eating, tearing off big hunks at a time. Brenwar grunted and almost smiled, trying to keep the juicy bird meat out of his beard.

"Say," I said to the barkeep, shoving a gold coin his way, "I'm in need of some *dragon* accessories."

The man glared at me and said, "I don't know a thing about that, and it's best you take such business elsewhere." He shoved the coin back

I shoved it back saying, "Beg your pardon, Sir. Then a bottle of wine will do."

He hesitated, took the coin, and pulled a bottle down from the top shelf, setting it down and pointing to the door. "Once it's gone—you're gone." His eyes grazed the pommel of my sword on my back. "No dragon talk in my place." He turned and left.

"Cripes!" Brenwar said, wiping his mouth on his sleeve. "Why don't you just scare off every dragon poacher in town? Why don't you go ask for some Orc accessories as well?" He glared at the orcs, still huddled in the corner, grunting with dissatisfaction over something.

I slapped him on the shoulder and said, "You eat and drink; I'll do the rest."

As we sat and gorged ourselves on bird meat and wine, I felt the tone in the room shifting. The patrons that sat near us began to fade away elsewhere. Many of the patrons seemed to stiffen, some leaving, and more notorious sorts arriving. The men began to bristle and brag, their comments of their exploits designed to catch my ear. Like most bad people, it seemed they didn't like me. Despite my rugged armor and attempt to blend in, I looked more than formidable. So far as I could tell, I was the tallest man in the room, my shoulders, arms and chest as knotted and broad as the rest. What they hadn't noticed about me before, they had noticed now. But I didn't come here looking for a fight. Or did I?

I tapped the big brute at the end of the bar on the shoulder.

"Do that again, and I'll cut off your hand," he warned.

"No doubt you would try," I said, smiling over at the fair-haired woman with the curious and inviting eyes. "I'm in need of dragon accessories."

"Get out of here!" He shoved me away.

Dragon accessories were a profitable business. A single scale was almost worth a piece of gold. Dragon teeth, scales, skin, claws and horns, whether they contained magic or not, were highly prized possessions that adorned many wealthy citizens. It was a practice that made me sick, seeing my kind displayed for fashion. Dragons were the same as the other races, but treated like something different. Of course, not all dragons were good, but most people viewed them all as bad.

I shoved him back.

"You touch me again; you'll be the one to lose your hands." No one shoves me around.

The fair-haired woman forced her way between us, pushing her angry man friend back with both hands, saying, "No blood here tonight." Then she whirled on me, poking her finger in my chest. "Go and sit down. I don't know what game you're playing, but I'll not stand for any talk of dragons. We fight for gold, not poach."

"I can see that now. But I pay well. Pardon me," I said with a slight bow, retaking my seat. *That ought to get them going,* I thought.

The man and woman warriors grumbled with each another, then departed, but she gave me one long look over her shoulder as they went. Now, me and Brenwar sat and waited. The barkeep continued to glower at me, but he didn't throw me out as long as we kept paying, and Brenwar was still eating and drinking. So I sat, noted all the scowls, and waited and waited and waited. I was a dragon, so waiting wasn't such a bad thing for me. But words travel faster than the wind sometimes. That's when two lizard men wandered in, both taller than me, crocodile green, dressed like men, and armored like soldiers. Their yellow eyes attached themselves to me first as they ripped their daggers out and charged.

CHAPTER 8

Lizard Men. Big, strong and fast, like me, expect not nearly as smart, but that didn't really matter when all they wanted to do was kill you.

I slung my barstool into one, cracking it into timbers over its head.

"Blasted reptile! Ye spilled my drink," Brenwar bellowed, clubbing another on its head with his tankard.

Slowed, but not stunned, the lizard sprang on top of me, driving me hard to the floor. I locked my fingers on its wrists as it tried to drive its dagger into my throat. Its red lizard tongue licked out as it hissed, angry and fateful. The lizard men weren't many in the world, usually pawns to greater evil, but effective pawns no less. I drove my knee up into its stomach with little effect as its blade strained inches above my neck.

"Dieeeesss, Dragonssss!" it said with a heave.

It felt like the veins were going to burst in my arms when I shoved back with all my strength. Over the sound of the blood rushing behind my ears, I could hear a rising clamor and more hissing voices. Not good. Yet Brenwar's bellows were clear.

"NO!" I yelled back. In a blink, I freed one hand and punched its long nose, rocking back its head.

Whap! Whap! Whap!

The lizard man jerked away from my stinging blows, but my hands felt like they were punching a wall. Still, lizard men hate getting hit in the nose, so do most lizards, for that matter. My blood was running hot now, the warrior in me suddenly alive as I jumped on its back and smashed its face into the floor. The dagger clattered from its grasp, and I snatched it up and rolled back to my feet.

Brenwar had the other one on the ground in a chokehold.

Crack!

And now it was dead, but the first two weren't the last. Three more were charging my way, not with daggers, but heavy broadswords this time. I can't imagine what I would have said that would have drawn so much attention.

Shing!

There was an audible gasp in the room as I whipped Fang's glowing blade through the air. Every eye was wide and wary, and I had to remember I had no friends here except Brenwar. The lizard men stopped for a moment, but they were well trained soldiers ordered to move forward.

The first lizard man charged past Brenwar, sword arcing downward and clashing hard into mine, juttering my arms.

Bap!

I punched its nose, rammed my knee in its gut, and jammed my sword into the thigh of the one behind it, drawing a pain filled hiss from its lizard lips. Two more were down, and the third had an angry dwarven man latched on its back. I raised my sword to deliver a lethal blow. I know, I know. My father warned me that killing is only a last resort, but I don't care what anyone says: lizard men and orcs don't count.

"Stop!" The Barkeep screamed. "STOP!"

No one moved, not even the lizard men.

Crack!

Well, that was one lizard man that wasn't going to move again for sure as Brenwar rode its dead body down to the floor.

"YOU, with the magic sword, get out of my TAVERN!"

"Me? But they attacked me!"

My longsword Fang hummed in my hand, its blade glimmering with a radiant light like the first crack of dawn. I brought the tip of its edge towards the barkeep's nose. I wasn't in any mood to be accused of something I didn't do.

He held his hands up, but tipped his chin up towards the folks behind me. I had a bad feeling as I turned to look. The two arm wrestlers stood now, each with a short sword in hand, eyes narrowed and ready to jump. The orcs, once three and now six, had drifted closer. The adventurers at the long table now stood. A staff glowed in one's hand, a sword glimmered in another. One warrior, grim faced and wearing chainmail, had a crossbow pointed at my chest. One woman, small and slender, stood poised on a chair, a handful of throwing knives bared. There were more, too, each focused on me, ready to fight or kill if need be.

"You can all try to take me if you want, but you won't all survive. Is your life worth the risk or not?" I glared back at the barkeep. "Your patrons can't pay if they're dead."

It was a bluff. I wouldn't have killed any of them, except the orcs. I swear they don't count. Neither do the lizard men, three of which had begun crawling back out the way they came. Lizard men and me didn't get along. We went way back. Well, I didn't mention it before, but I've been around awhile, and when you live a long time and do what I do, you tend to make enemies. I had plenty to go around. Chances were that one of my enemies knew I was here and had sent in a squadron of goons to kill me.

"Just go," the bartender pleaded, his eyes nervous now.

I looked at the two dead lizard men on the floor and asked, "What about them?"

"I'll take care of them. The lizards don't hold any worth with the authorities."

Brenwar had resumed his eating, his blocky mailed shoulder hunched back over his pheasant. I was still itching for a fight.

The tension in the air had not slackened. My legs were still ready to spring. That's when the man in the corner stood up and walked towards the center of the room. Long and gaunt, hooded in a dark cloak, he seemed more of a ghost than a man. All eyes now fell on the man that held a hefty sack in one hand and dropped it on the table to the sound of clinking coins.

Slowly, he pulled his hood back, revealing a shaven head that was tattooed with symbols and signs I knew all too well. He was a cleric of Barnabus, a cult of men obsessed with the dragons. Meddlers in a dark and ancient magic. I hadn't expected to come across one so soon. His voice was loud and raspy as he pointed at me and said:

"This bag of gold to the one that brings me his head!"

Clatch-Zip!

A crossbow bolt darted towards my ducking head and caught the barkeep full in the shoulder.

"What!" Brenwar roared, readying his dwarven war hammer, sharp at one end, like an anvil on the other.

"Don't let that cleric escape, Brenwar!" I said, smacking the muscled goons' blades with Fang. I clipped one in the leg and took a rock hard shot in the jaw from the other. He gloated. I retaliated, cracking him upside his skull with the flat of my blade.

"Agh!" I cried out in pain. A row of small knives were imbedded in my arm, courtesy of the little rogue woman. I'd have to deal with her later. I had to get the cleric, who was scurrying away towards the door. Brenwar was a barricade at the door, a host of orcs swarming at him.

"Let's dance, you smelly beasts!" he yelled, hitting one so hard it toppled the others.

He could handle himself, and I had bigger problems: the party of adventurers had surrounded me. Well, mercenaries seemed to be more likely the term for them.

I leapt back as the lanky fighter with the brilliant sword tried to cut me in half. He was a young man, confident in his skills.

Clang! Clang! Clatter!

He lacked my power or speed as I tore his sword free from his grasp.

Slice!

I clipped muscle from his sword arm and sent him spinning to the floor.

Then everything went wrong.

The little woman jammed a dagger in my back. The wizard fired a handful of missiles into my chest, and the crossbowman, now wielding a hammer, slung it into my chest. That's why I wear armor, forged by the dwarves at that. My breastplate had saved me from dying more than a dozen times, but I'd gotten careless. I should have negotiated with this hardy brood, but I wanted to fight instead. I was mad. I was Nath Dragon, the greatest hero in the land, as far as I was concerned. It was time they saw that.

I banged the tip of my sword on the hard oaken floor. The metal hummed and vibrated with power.

THAAAAROOOOONG!!!

Glass shattered. Men and women fell to the floor, covering their ears, all except me and Brenwar, who stood on top of a pile of what looked to be dead orcs. I could see him yelling at me, but I could not hear. His lips mouthed the words, "Shut that sword off!"

I sheathed my singing blade, and the sound stopped immediately. The entire tavern looked like it had been turned upside down. Everyone living was moaning or wailing. The loudest among them? The Cleric of Barnabus. Huddled up in a fetal position, shivering like a leaf.

Fang's power was pretty helpful when it came to ending a fight with no one dying, but it didn't work on every race, or most of the time, for that matter. Fang only did what it wanted to do. My father said the sword had a mind of its own, and I was pretty sure that was true. I grabbed the cleric by the collar of his robe and dragged him over the bar. Brenwar had the cleric's bag of gold in his hand when he came off and plopped it on the bar. The barkeep, grimacing in pain from the crossbow bolt in his shoulder that was meant for me, smiled as the dwarf filled his hands with the gold and spilled them on the bar. "Fer the damages. The rest I'll be keeping."

"So long," I said, tying and gagging the cleric and hoisting him over my shoulder. "And thanks. This man will have just what I'm looking for."

The remaining patrons, still dazed and confused, holding their heads and stomachs, paid no mind at all as I left. They should have learned a lesson today: never pick a fight with an opponent you don't know anything about; it just might be a dragon.

CHAPTER 9

No one outside seemed to mind as we pushed our way through the bewildered crowd of the neighborhood, loaded our prisoner on my horse, and galloped towards a part of town I knew better. The authorities weren't likely to give much chase, if they even bothered at all. Some parts of the city were void of the common rules of order.

"Here," I said to Brenwar, turning my steed inside a large barn of stables.

A stable hand, a young man, straw colored hair, and sandaled, greeted us with an eerie glance at my wriggling captive.

"No questions," I said, handing him a few coins.

"No problem," he said with a smile as broad as an ogre's back.

Stables and barns are good places to do business, or interrogations, for that matter. No echoes, and the smell of manure tends to offend most people, keeps them away. I shoved the cleric from my saddle, and Brenwar dragged him inside the stables over the straw and stood watch outside.

As I said, the Clerics of Barnabus are an evil lot, and we go way back. The fact that one had already come after me was a stroke of luck, both good and bad. Bad, because they almost got me killed. Good, because this man would lead me to their next nefarious plot. Normally, some desperate person would tell me something or find someone that would, when I asked after dragon articles. I'd follow their information, and sometimes that led to a dead end, but oft times it led me to where I was going. The Clerics of Barnabus, it seemed, had become privy to my ways. And when it came to dragons, they had eyes and ears everywhere.

From then on, I had to be more careful how I went about gathering information.

Now the hard part. Interrogation. Taking information from an unwilling mind by force. It wasn't a very dragon-like way of doing things, but it didn't always have to be brutal.

I pinned the man up against the wall by the neck and jerked the rag from his mouth. His impulse to scream was cut short as my fingers squeezed around his throat.

"Urk!"

"That's a good little evil cleric. Keep quiet, and I'll let you breathe." I squeezed a little harder, forcing his eyes open wider. "I talk. You answer, quietly. Understand?"

He blinked.

That was pretty much all he could do, and I took it as a definitive yes. I could tell by the tattoos on his head that this acolyte was only a few notches above a lackey of the cult. He had some magic, but nothing I couldn't handle.

"See my dwarven friend over there?" I said.

Brenwar peered inside, holding a manure shovel in his hand.

"Look at what he does to people that don't cooperate."

He took the shovel, blacksmith hands holding both ends of the wooden handle, and grunted.

Snap!

The skin on the cleric's already gaunt face paled. His eyes blinked rapidly.

"Now, I'd say that shovel's thicker than your skinny bones. So, I suggest you answer my questions, in detail, or you'll be going home in a wheelbarrow."

The man's chin quivered. I couldn't ask for a better result.

"Y-You're, you're N-Nath Dragon. Aren't you?"

"You didn't know that already?"

"I was told it was you, but I did not believe until I saw for myself. Someone mentioned you'd come into town. I followed you in. Fully ready to see you dead. There is such a high bounty on your head. But, you move so fast. Impossible. Unnatural. I knew I'd lost as soon as it started, but I had no choice but to try," he said grinning sheepishly.

I slapped him in the face.

"Please, no flattery if you want to walk again."

Evil ones always try to beguile and convince a person their distorted intentions are only for the best, or out of necessity. It's tough to sell me if you're a man, but an attractive woman is a different story, and I knew right there and then I had best be more careful.

"We hate you, Nath Dragon! We'll have your head by dawn!"

"My, it seems you've forgotten what happened to my dear friend and the shovel. Brenwar!"

"No!" The evil cleric pleaded. "No. I can't have my arms and legs splintered. I'd rather die. Make a deal with me."

"No."

"Hear me out. I know where many dragons are kept, near this city. Small ones."

He had my attention. The little ones, some as small as hawks, others bigger than dogs, weren't easy to catch, but easy to keep. The thought of them being caged infuriated me. I pushed harder on his throat.

"You tell me now, and not a single bone of yours will be broken."

He nodded. I eased the pressure.

"Take the trail to Orcen Hold."

***

Finnius the Cleric of Barnabus lived, and Nath Dragon and his dwarven companion, Brenwar, were long gone. But still he struggled in his bindings, and his knee throbbed like an angry heart where the dwarf had whacked him with the busted shovel.

"Let me help you with that," a woman said. Her dark grey robes matched his, but she had short raven-colored hair, and thin lips of a pale purple.

She pulled the gag from his mouth and helped him to his feet.

"Have you done well, acolyte Finnius?" she asked, cutting the bonds from his wrists.

"I did exactly as you ordered, High Priestess." He rubbed his reddened wrists. "They are halfway to Orcen Hold by now. Your plan, Priestess, I'm certain will be successful. In a few more hours, Nath Dragon will be ours."

She rubbed her hand over his bald head and smiled.

"You'll be needing more tattoos after this, Finnius. I had my doubts you would pull this off, but it seems you did quite well. Assuming, of course, they arrive as expected."

"Oh they will, Priestess. Nath's eyes were as fierce as a dragon's when I said it. He'll not be stopped."

She walked away and said, "That's what I'm counting on. This day, the Clerics of Barnabus will forever change the life of Nath Dragon."

Finnius limped along behind her toward the front of the stables, where the stablehand greeted her from a distance. A long serpent's tail slipped out from underneath her robes. Striking like a snake, it knocked the boy clear from his feet, smacking him hard into the wall. Finnius swallowed hard and hurried along.

CHAPTER 10

Orcen Hold. Not nearly as bad as it sounds, but still bad, miles north east from Narnum towards the orcen city of Thraagamor. It's a stronghold, filled with brigands and mercenaries, all swords and daggers for hire that sometimes form an army whose side you never know they were on.

It isn't just orcs, either, or even mostly orcs for that matter, but men and some of the other races as well. The name most likely kept unwanted do-gooders like me away. I'd never been there before, but the world was vast, and even in my centuries of life, I still couldn't have been everywhere. That would still take some time.

Brenwar and I rode our mounts up a steep road that winded up a hillside, rather than around it, which would have been wholly more adequate. On the crest of the hill, no more than a mile high, I could see there was a massive fort of wood posts and block, jutting into the darkening sky. Pigeons scattered in the air, wings flapping before settling back along the edges of the walls. Pigeons are crumb snatching carrion, never a good sign, rather a bad one, as the black and white speckled birds are drawn to filth. Of course, what would one expect from a place named Orcen Hold?

I pulled my hood over my head as the drizzling rain became a heavy down pour, soaking me to the bone in less than a minute. I hated being wet, or drenched, or saturated in any kind of water that I hadn't planned on. You'd think a tough man like me would be used to it by now, but I saw no reason to like it. I like the sun, the heat on my face, the sweat glistening on my skin.

As the horses clopped through the mud, we made our way around the last bend, stopped, and looked up. Orcen Hold was a good bit bigger than it had looked from below. A veritable city that could host thousands, where I assumed at most were just a few hundred. Well-fortified, there were watch towers along the walls, soldiers spread out, crossbows ready to cut any unwanted intruders down. Ahead, the main gate, two twenty foot high doors, stood open behind a small moat. I couldn't shed the foreboding feeling that overcame me any more easily than the water soaking my back. It didn't seem like the kind of place where two men entered and got to leave... alive, anyway.

Still, we trotted over the draw bridge, through the doors, and underneath the portcullis that hung over us like a massive set of iron jaws.

"Yer sure ye want to do this?" Brenwar's beard was dripping with rain.

"I'd do just about anything to get us out of this rain."

Behind the walls over Orcen Hold lay a small city, not refined, but functional. The roads, normally covered with brick and stone customary of most cities, were dirt, now turned to mud. The buildings, ramshackle and ruddy, were tucked neatly behind plank wood walkways. People were milling about, dashing through puddles and across the streets from one porch to the other. Some shouted back and forth, in arguments of some sort. The children, possibly the most mottled ones I'd ever seen, played in the mud, their faces, grimy, poor, and hungry. And the smell. I could only assume it would have been worse without the rain, so for a moment I was thankful for the rain.

The Troll's Toe. That was the place we were looking for. The Cleric of Barnabus, Finnius was his name, had proven to be a very unwilling participant after he let loose the location called Orcen Hold. His tongue had frozen in his clenched jaws. A well placed spade to the knee, courtesy of Brenwar, and he'd told me what I was certain I needed to know.

The light was dim as the sinking sun continued to dip behind the clouds and disappear, turning an otherwise hot day cold. The wind began to bang the wooden signs that hung from chains in front of the buildings, making the dreary trek from an unknown city worse.

The firelight that gleamed from behind the dingy windows was a welcoming sight despite the coarse faces that glared at us with more remorse than curiosity. Blasted orcs. If it weren't for them, I swear that life on Nalzambor would be an excellent party.

"There," Brenwar said, pointing his stubby finger in the rain. "Seems we've found what yer looking for. But Nath, it's not too late to turn back. I'd say we're outnumbered here, uh, about a thousand to one."

"I thought you liked those kinds of odds?" I said, trying to wipe the rain from my face.

"Er ... well, I do. But, this place reeks. If I'm to die, I'd like it to be somewhere a little closer to my home."

"Die?"

Brenwar looked a little bit ashamed when he said, "I just want to make sure I get a proper funeral. I'll not have a bunch of orcs burying me in the sewer. Or you, either, for that matter."

Brenwar was a bit obsessive about his funeral. It's a special thing for a dwarf. If they had their way, they'd die in battle, but they just wanted to be remembered for it. Brenwar, an older man by dwarven standards, had lived longer than even me and more than likely had a couple hundred years to go. He'd been with me so long, it didn't seem that he could ever die. But I'd seen other dwarves as great as him perish before.

The wind picked up, banging the sign to the Troll's Toe hard against the rickety building frame as we hitched our horses and went inside. Warm air and the smell of bread dough and stale ale greeted us as we sat down at a small table away from the firelight. The crowded room was momentarily quiet, more on account of Brenwar's presence than mine. It wasn't often you saw a dwarf in Orcen Hold, but Brenwar's bushy bearded face wasn't the only one. Still, I couldn't shake the feeling we were all on our own.

CHAPTER 11

It was a rough bunch, as bad as I'd ever seen. Tattooed, scarred, ornery, peg-legged, eye-patched, and hook-handed, it looked like the perfect place to get in trouble. The men were as coarse and rude as the orcs and half-orcs that snorted and blustered around the bar. The women were as crass as the men, singing and dancing on a small stage, their voices as soothing as a glass of boiling water.

"Now what?" Brenwar asked, looking back over his shoulder.

"We wait," I said, waving over a waitress with hips as big as an ogre's.

"What will it be, weary travelers?" She had a gap-toothed smile.

"Two of whatever tastes best with your ale," Brenwar spouted. "Human food, not the orcen mishmash that tastes like mud and worms."

She tried to make a pretty smile, but it was quite frightening when she said, "As you wish, Dwarven Sire."

"I think she likes you," I said.

"I certainly don't see why she wouldn't," he said, watching her prance away.

I sat there, sulking and soaking, damp hood still covering my face. It wasn't as if anyone would recognize me, but I'd still stick out like a sore thumb. There was something about my eyes and looks that drew stares, and for the most part, I like that kind of attention, but here, it was the kind of attention I didn't want. I just needed to lay low and wait until the opportunity presented itself. In a pain-filled voice, Finnius had assured us that I would know.

My appetite was barren, but the food wasn't half bad as I sat there and picked at it. Something about the greasy meat and cheeses they served in the worst of places always made me want to come back for more. It was getting late though, less than an hour from the middle of the night, and my wet clothes finally began to dry. The rain no longer splattered on the window panes, and I could again see the moon's hazy glow. I craned my neck at the chatter about dragons that lingered in the air, but it was hard to make anything out over all the singing voices and carousing.

Brenwar nudged me, pointing over towards a mousy man with hunched shoulders whispering among the tables. I watched him, his lips flapping in a feverish and convincing fashion. Some shoved him away, while others minded his words with keen interest. He had my interest as well. *Dragons.* I could see the word on his lips as plain as the nose on his face. I wasn't a lip reader or mind reader, but when it came to anything about dragons I could just tell.

Like a busy rodent, he darted from one table to the next, collecting coins and scowls, while directing the people towards the back of the room where I watched them disappear behind the fireplace mantle. *Don't ask for it. Wait for it.* That's what the cleric Finnius had said. It made sense, too. Asking would only rouse suspicion.

"You think he'll make it our way or not?" Brenwar combed some food from his beard.

The little man's head popped up our way, as if he'd heard Brenwar's question. He scurried towards us, his ferret face nervous, eyes prying into the shadows beneath my hood. Brenwar shoved him back a step.

"Some privacy, Man."

The small man hissed a little, then spoke fast.

"Dragon fights. Five gold. Dragon Fights. Five gold. Last chance. One.

Two.Three …" his fingers were collapsing on his hand. "Four. Fi—"

"Sure," I said, sliding the coins over the table.

He frowned.

"Five for you!" he said, offended, scowling at Brenwar. "Seven for the dwarf!"

"Why you little—", Brenwar made a fist.

"Six," I insisted. You have to barter with dealers like these or else they won't respect you, and that can lead to trouble.

"Fine," he said, snatching the additional coins I pushed his way. He left two tokens, each wooden with a dragon face carved into it. "Under thirty minutes. Be late and no see."

I looked over at Brenwar as the little wispy-haired man left and said, "I suppose we should go, then."

Brenwar finished off the last of his ale and wiped his mouth.

"I suppose," he said, casting an odd look over at the large stone fireplace. "It's underground, it is. I feel the draft and the shifting of the stones. We're over a cave, or something carved from the mountain. Bad work. Not dwarven." He got up and patted his belly. "Probably collapse on us, it will. They probably let the orcs build the tunnel."

"You'll dig us out if it does, won't you?" I followed him behind the mantle. He didn't say a word.

One thing about Nalzambor, there were always new places to go. It was impossible to ever see what was behind every door in every city, and for the most part it was exciting. The chill from the damp clothes and biting air had worn off now, and the hearth of the stone fireplace was like a warm summer day. I put my hand on the rock, nice and toasty, which made me think of when I used to lie alongside my father's belly when I was a boy. He'd tell the most excellent stories, and even though they usually lasted more than a week, I never got bored of them.

We followed a man and woman of questionable character down a narrow winding stairwell.

"Bah. Orcen engineers. There should be no such thing," Brenwar complained, his heavy feet thundering down the steps.

At the bottom, two half-orcen men waited, armored in chainmail from head to toe, and two more stood behind them, spears at the ready. The the tips of my fingers tingled. I realized I still had my sword, and Brenwar his war axe, but the pair before us, with steel swinging on their hips, paid their tokens and moved on, down a tunnel where many loud voices were shouting. The half-orcen man snatched my token from my hand and sneered.

"Take down your hood."

Brenwar stiffened at my side, hands clutching his weapon with white knuckles.

I looked down into the half-orcen eyes and growled, "I paid my share. No one said hoods weren't allowed. You have something against hoods?"

His lip curled back, but he couldn't tear his eyes away. I wouldn't let him. I looked deeper into him. I could see his hate and fear. There was little good in him, but enough man left for him to step aside.

"Go ahead," he said, blinking hard and moving on to the next people.

Making our way down the tunnel cut through the rock, I could feel the cool draft air nipping at my sweating neck. The sound of voices was getting louder now. A mix of races I could hear. Men mostly, but orcs, too, and a few dwarves as well. We emerged into a cavernous room, part cave, part auditorium, with seats carved from stone that formed a crude arena. The excited voices were shouting at a shimmering black curtain that covered an object in the center about twenty feet high and thirty feet wide.

The hair on my neck stiffened as I pushed my way through the crowd that circled and pressed around the wall that surrounded it.

"Kill the dragon!" someone cried, jostling my senses.

An outcry of agreement followed, along with a series of cheers. I could feel more bodies pressing against mine, a frenzied and gambling hoard. From above, a powerful voice, amplified beyond the powers of nature, shouted out.

"SILENCE!"

I'd never seen so many loud and obnoxious people fall silent at once, yet they did, looking upward at the sound of the voice. A man, as tall as he was wide, stood in robes laced in arcane symbols, glittering different colors in the light. A dragon's claw, a big one, jostled around his fat neck as he ran his pudgy fingers through a mop of brown hair. He seemed tired, expressionless, and bored. He yawned, his mouth opening three times bigger than it looked.

Brenwar nudged me, saying, "That ain't no man."

Whatever he was, he kept on speaking.

"SILENCE!"

He said it once again, long and drawn out. At this rate, I'd never see what was underneath the curtain.

"LET ... THE ... DRAGON ... GAMES ... BEEEEEEE ... GIIIIIN!"

There was a clap of thunder and a flash of light, followed by a series of gasps.

I gawped at what I saw next. A cage. A series of iron works constructed into a see-through dome of metal. But that wasn't what got me. I'd seen plenty of cages before. Instead, it was who was perched inside on a swing. A dragon, no taller than a dwarf, glimmering with orange and yellow scales, clawed wings covering his face and body. He shone like a diamond inside a room full of coal. My nerves turned to sheets of ice when the big fat man said.

"SEND ... IN ... THE ... TROLLS!"

CHAPTER 12

It seemed so out of place to imagine such things as trolls fighting a dragon, albeit a small one, to the death. My inner self was recoiling, uncertain what to do, when the cage doors opened on a tunnel, to a rousing course of cheers. A troll—ten kinds of ugly all wrapped up into a ruddy piece of brawny flesh towering at ten feet tall—stood there, pounding its fist into its hand. The smacking was so loud it popped my ears. I tore my eyes away from the troll that lumbered, arms swinging into the walls, shaking the cage on its way into the chamber. The dragon was as still as a crane on his perch, unmoving. *Good boy,* I thought. I could tell he was a boy by the scales on his belly, a little darker than the orange and yellow scales on his body, unlike the girls, who were usually lighter than the rest.

The troll, naked except for a burlap loin cloth, narrowed its small eyes on the dragon and let out a terrible yell, loud and getting louder. A battle cry of sorts. A chorus of bestial fury. The dragon remained at peace on his perch, not showing the slightest degree of motion.

The crowed quieted. All eyes as full as the moon and fixated on the dragon. My own heart was pounding in my chest like a team of galloping horses. The troll, every bit as dangerous as it was dumb, lumbered around the dragon, like a predator sizing up its prey. Despite their lack of intelligence, trolls aren't impulsive, but once they make a decision, which usually involves something other than them dying, they stick to it.

"What's going on?" Brenwar muttered.

"I'm not sure."

"KILL THE DRAGON!" someone cried.

That's when the chants began, a rising crescendo of fury, and like a frenzied ape the troll beat its chest, charging the unmoving dragon, massive fists raised up and ready to deal a lethal blow.

The dragon's wings popped open, his serpentine neck striking out as he began breathing a stream of white lava.

The troll screamed in agony, thrashing under the weight of the dragon's breath that coated it from head to toe with brilliant white burning oil. The troll's flesh charred and smoked, its efforts to escape diminishing. The heat was like sticking your face too close to a campfire, from where I stood. The crowd roared so loud I couldn't hear myself think. I slapped Brenwar on the back, unable to hide my elation as the little dragon finished, leaving nothing left of the troll but the smoldering bones and an uncanny stink.

Brenwar looked up at me, eyes as big as stones, and said, "Did you see that? I've never seen a dragon with breath like that!"

Dragons. There were all kinds. Different makes and families, and each kind had a special weapon or two of its own. The orange dragons, called Ruffies, were one of the noblest and deadliest of them all. I had to get this one out, and out soon. He was still young, and it would be at least a day before his breath returned.

"That should do it," I said. "Let's stick around and see what we can do to sneak this dragon out of here."

There was a lot of murmuring, most good, some bad. It seemed most of the people that liked to take chances had been smart enough to bet on the dragon. I was expecting everyone to leave, but most of them were sticking around and talking. Of course, how often do you get to see a live dragon fight? Their fascination sickened me.

I looked above as the fat man whose mouth was too large for his face spoke again.

SEND … IN … MORE … TROLLS!

My heart sunk down into my toes. "What?" I couldn't hide my exclamation. Wooden double doors opened on the other side of the cage into the tunnel again. Two trolls, this time carrying shields, clubs and wearing helmets, charged the orange dragon on the perch. The crowd screamed. I screamed. The dragon didn't stand a chance. He'd last another minute or two at most.

"We've got to get him out of there, Brenwar!" I yelled.

The dragon zoomed from his perch, dashing between the legs of one troll who swung, missed and bashed the other. Dragons are fast, no matter how big they are. But no dragon with spent breath and little room to fly could last for long in that cage.

"Find a way in, Brenwar!"

As soon as I pushed one person away, two more appeared. The crowd was in a frenzy, trying to get a closer look. The cage, so far as I could see, didn't have a door or opening except into the tunnel on the other side. I heard a sound like a rattle snake's rattle. The Ruffie clawed his way up one troll's back, tearing its flesh up like dirt, drawing an inhuman howl. He perched on one troll's head and taunted the other with the rattle snake sound made by tiny fins that buzzed by his ears.

WANG!

One troll struck the other on its metal helmet just as the dragon darted away. It looked like two clumsy dogs trying to catch a mouse. One troll would swing, miss, and hit the other. That wouldn't last forever. Dragons, for all their speed and skill, tire quickly after their dragon breath is spent. They are magic, and magic needs time to recharge. Trolls, however, tire about as easily as a wall of stone. Those two wouldn't stop or slow until they were dead.

"Brenwar!"

I couldn't see him, but I could see people falling like stones, a path of people parting within the throng before closing up again.

The voice from above came again.

"STOP ... THEM!"

I saw him, the fat mage, like a toad on a stool, pointing straight at me. The crowd, dazzled by the spectacular fight, gave the man little notice, but the guards, the ones armed to the teeth, they were ready and coming after me. If they got me, I'd never get to the dragon in time, and I still hadn't figured out a way inside the cage.

"MOVE!" I shouted, but the people paid me no mind.

That's when I heard it, an awful sound, the sound of a dragon crying out, his shrieking so loud it hurt my ears . A troll had ahold of his wing. The dragon fought and fluttered, talons tearing into the troll's flesh, but its grip held firm. That's when something snapped inside me. A geyser of power erupted within my bones. Fang, my sword, was glowing white hot in my hands. I was surrounded, but my mind was no longer my own. The guards and men were falling under the wrath of my blade. I ignored the fear-filled screams and howls of fury. I could not tell one man from another. All I wanted to do was save the dragon, and nothing was going to stop me.

There was blood and fury in my eyes as I swung Fang into the iron cage. Fang cut into the iron as I chopped like a lumberjack gone mad. *Hack! Hack! Hack!* I was through, a troll's massive back awaiting me. I sent Fang through its spine and caught a glimmer of the dragon slithering away. Brenwar was yelling. I turned in time to see the other troll's club coming for me. I dove. *Whump!* The club missed my head. I rolled. *Whump!* It almost broke my back as I scrambled away. *Crack!* The troll fell over dead, thanks to the help of Brenwar's war hammer catching it in the skull.

"Come on!" He pulled me to my feet. Ahead, the large wooden double doors, at least ten inches thick, barred our escape from the coming wrath of who knows what.

Brenwar charged, war-hammer raised over his head, bellowing, "BARTFAAAAST!"

There was a clap of thunder, the splintering of wood, and a giant hole in the doors that had momentarily barred our path. The dragon was gone like a bolt of orange lightning.

"Follow that dragon," I yelled, following Brenwar down the tunnel.

The dwarven fighter's short legs churned like a billy goat's as he charged down one tunnel and through another. My instincts fired at the sound of armored soldiers coming after us down the tunnel.

"Do you know where you're going, Brenwar?" I cried from behind him.

Brenwar snorted, "I'm a dwarf, aren't I? Not a tunnel made that can lose me."

We found ourselves running down a long corridor, where a wooden door had been busted open that led outside into the pouring rain. The pounding of armored boot steps was coming our way, barking orders and calling for our heads. It was time to make a stand.

A group of heavily armed soldiers rounded the corner, armored in chainmail from head to toe, the silver tips of their spears glinting in the torch light.

"Get him," one ordered from behind, thrusting his sword in the air.

I whipped Fang's keen edge around my body and yelled back.

"The first one that comes within ten feet of me is dead!"

The soldiers stopped, looking with uncertainty towards one another. That's when I noticed the blood dripping from my sword. Their eyes were on it as well, and a hollow feeling crept over me. How many had I killed? Everything was a blur. Perhaps it was troll's blood, but it didn't' seem dark enough.

"Skewer that man!" The commander's face was red. "If you don't follow orders, then you're dead men anyway. We've got strength in numbers. Attack!"

The first two spearmen lowered their weapons at my belly and advanced. All I wanted to do was buy time. Just a few seconds more. I leaped in, batting one spear away with my sword and yanking the spear away from the next man. The soldiers shuffled back. Now I faced them with a sword in one hand and a spear hoisted over my shoulder.

"The next soldier to advance will catch this in his belly," I said, motioning with the spear.

"Cowards! Charge him! Charge him now!"

The unarmed spearman stepped back as another took his place.

I launched my spear into his leg. The man let out a cry of pain as he tumbled to the ground.

I ducked as a spear whizzed past my face.

"Charge!"

I hoisted Fang over my head and said, "Stop! I surrender!"

No one moved, every eye intent on me.

The commander shouted from the back, "Drop your sword, then!"

Slowly, I lowered my arms. But I had another plan. I'd use Fang's magic to blast back my enemies as I'd done in the tavern.

"What are you smiling for?" The commander moved forward.

"I'm just glad to put an end to the violence, is all. Oh, and you might want to hold your ears."

"What for?"

I banged the tip of Fang's blade on the stone corridor's floor.

Ting.

Nothing happened. I tried it again.

Ting.

Drat!

"Fang, what are you doing?" I shook my sword.

The commander was not amused. "You going to drop that sword, or not?"

I was flat-footed now with nowhere to go but out. I grasped my sword in both my hands and pulled it in front of my face.

"I've changed my mind. I'm going to fight you all. To the death!" I let out a battle cry and charged forward. All of the soldiers hunkered down. In stride, I pivoted on my right foot, twisted the other way, and dashed outside the busted doorway into the rain.

I was drenched the moment I made it out into the river of mud that was supposed to be a street. I heard a horse nicker nearby and dashed that way. Brenwar, my horse in tow, was galloping down the road, hooves splashing in the water.

"Run, Dragon!"

The heavy boots were trampling behind me as I sprinted alongside Brenwar, grabbed ahold of the saddle on my horse, and pulled myself up.

"Great timing," I yelled up towards Brenwar as we began our gallop away. "I couldn't have done better myself—*ulp*!"

Something that burned like fire slammed into my back. Another spear sailed past my head, followed by another. The pain was excruciating as I galloped onward with a spear in my back, holding on for dear life.

***

It was dawn before we stopped riding. I could barely keep my head up, and I swore I'd black out any second. We didn't slow, not once, taking trails little known to most. I'd been that certain our pursuers were many. I was restless when we stopped along a silvery stream and gave the horses a moment to drink.

"Finally stopping are we? Think we lost them?" Brenwar said.

I slid from my saddle, grimacing.

"What's the matter with you, Nath? You look like … Egad! Is that a spear in your back?"

He hurried over and inspected my wound.

"Ouch! I don't need speared again, Brenwar!"

"Why didn't you say something, you fool! You could've bled to death."

"It's not that bad," I gasped. "Only a javelin, right?"

"Sure, and I'm a fairy's uncle. Still, it's a small one. Not barbed for hunting. It's wedged between your armor and your back. Hold this." Brenwar put my horse reins in my mouth.

"What for," I tried to say.

"Just bite down. I've got to pull the spear out."

I shook my head.

Brenwar yanked out the spear. I screamed. It felt like my entire back was pulled out, and I fell to my knees.

"I'm going to need to stitch that up. And quick. Are you sure you are feeling sound? That's a dangerous wound. Another inch it'd be inside a lung."

It hurt, but I'd been stitched up by Brenwar before. Besides, I had some salve that would accelerate the healing.

"All done," he grumbled as he poked his finger in my face, "and next time, tell me something."

"Thanks, Brenwar." I rolled my shoulder, and my back still burned like fire. At least the rain had passed.

"You sure you're feeling well? You don't look well."

"I've been recently skewered. I'd assume that's it."

"Pah ... Yer fine, I guess," he said, walking away.

The sun, warm on my face, a feeling that normally gave me comfort, gave me none. Brenwar, usually full of boasts after a battle, was quiet. I picked up a stone and skipped it from my side of the stream to the other.

"Another dragon saved," I said. "A fairly powerful Ruffie, at that."

"Aye," Brenwar said, refilling his canteen. "Some fight, too. Works up the ole' appetite, it does." He thumped his armored belly with his fist. "How about I snare a rabbit or two?"

"I've got my bow."

"Are ye daft? Ye didn't bring yer bow," he argued, his busy face widening with worry.

"What?" I said, "You look like you just swallowed a halfling. Brenwar ..."

The world wobbled beneath me. Bright spots burst in my eyes: pink, green and yellow. Brenwar's arms stretched and stretched and stretched toward me, beyond me. His face spun like a pinwheel and was gone. Silence. Blackness. I fell, I think.

***

Finnius stood alongside the high priestess of the Clerics of Barnabus with a nervous look in his rodent eyes. He'd seen men dead before, but not so many, not like this. He couldn't imagine how Nath Dragon had done all this, but the witnesses, the ones that survived the horror, assured him he had. The arena beneath the Troll's Toe in Orcen Hold looked like a battlefield. A battle that they had clearly lost, not to mention losing a dragon as well. The high priestess, however, didn't seem worried. Arms folded over her chest, a dark twinkle in her eyes, a smile cropping up from the corner of her mouth, she said, "It won't be long, Finnius. Nath Dragon will be mine."

CHAPTER 13

It was dark. I smelled burning wood. Meat roasting over a fire. My eyes opened to a brilliant starlit sky, and I felt whole again. I rolled over to where a campfire blazed and Brenwar kneeled, turning rabbit meat on a spit.

"Dinner time already?" I got up and walked over.

Brenwar looked at me like I'd come back from the dead.

"What? Has it been a day or more? You look like I've been sleeping for a week." I stretched my arms out and yawned. "I must admit though, it feels like I've slept for a week, maybe longer. I guess saving dragons is bound to catch up with you."

"Or turning into one," he said. At least, I thought that was what he said.

"Brenwar, is that some kind of joke?"

I looked at him, the sky, and the moon before turning back towards the stream that was no longer there. A very bad feeling overcame me, like a part of my life was missing.

"Say, how'd I get here? Where's the water? Brenwar, how long have I been out?"

He mumbled something.

"Louder," I insisted.

"Three months! Three months, Nath Dragon! And I've been out here counting daisies and trapping furry little animals." He rose to his feet and poked me in the chest. "Now, three months isn't long for a dwarf, but it's not short by any measure, either."

"Why didn't you wake me, then?"

He jumped up on his feet and yelled, "Don't you think I tried? I could've set you on fire, and you wouldn't have moved! I should have let the harpies carry you off."

"Harpies?"

"Pah," he said, waving me off.

I raked my fingers through my hair and checked the beard that had grown on my face. I scratched it with my nails that were unusually long, on my right hand anyway. I held my hand out and stared. Brenwar's downcast face stayed down, kicking at the dirt as I looked at the black scales on the fingers of my dragon-like hand.

"Gagh!" I said, jumping away from myself.

I looked at my other hand, the left, and it was fine, but my right—black glimmering scales and thick yellow claws like my father's—was a thing of beauty. A rush of energy and excitement went through me as I jumped high in the air and screamed with delight. I felt like a child again.

"I can go home again, Brenwar! I've gotten my scales! Or some scales."

I ran my new and old fingers over my face.

"Brenwar, is my face unchanged?"
He nodded.

I was relieved, but I wasn't certain whether I should have been or not. I shed the blanket from my shoulder, and everything but my right arm was fine, or human at least, and I still wasn't sure if that was a good thing or not. I checked behind me.

"Do I have a tail?'

"No!"

"Why so glum then, Brenwar? I've gotten scales!" I said, marveling at my arm.

He shrugged and said, "Don't know."

He was being stubborn, naturally, but something bothered me.

"What?"

"I ain't seen no man become a dragon before," he said, taking the rabbit from the spit. "Hungry?"

I gazed at my arm, its diamond-like scales shimmering in the twilight, like broken pieces of coal. I could feel power, true power, like I'd never felt before. I swore my right arm was twice as strong as my left, and my left was already stronger than most men's.

"Come, then, Brenwar! I can't wait a moment longer. It's time to go see my father!"

"So be it then, Nath."

***

The trek through the Sulfur Marsh at the bottom of the Mountain of Doom had never gone quicker as Brenwar and I made our way through the secret passageway. Most of the time, when I came home I was either half-dead, which had been the case the last time, or filled with dread because I had not gained any scales. Despite my father's and my disagreements over the past two centuries, I never wanted to disappoint him. This time, however, I had the upper hand. I had my scales, and my days as a man were numbered.

I took a moment to pause in reflection as I stood outside my father's chamber doors. The detail in the doors and the rest of the caves and tunnels appeared to have a greater meaning to me now. The brass framework interwoven in ornate patterns on the wooden doors said something to me. The symbols carried power.

"So," Brenwar's gruff voice interrupted my thoughts, "are you goin' inside, or are you going to stand there and gawk? It's a dwarven door, you know. You'd think you'd never seen it before." His thick fingers were playing with his beard. He seemed nervous, if that was at all possible.

"It's fine work. I just never noticed before. Do you think I should knock?"

"There's a first time for everything."

True, in all my years, I hadn't bothered to knock before. I wasn't certain why it was different this time, but it was. This time, of all times, the little things seemed to matter.

I looked down at Brenwar's face, then at the door, and lifted my fist to knock. Both doors swung open on their own.

"ENTER, SON, AND MY FRIEND THE DWARF."

I led, my chin held high, like the time I'd saved my first dragon. I felt like a boy again, new and refreshed, a spring in my step because the hard feelings at failed efforts were gone.

My father, the grandest dragon of them all, sat on his throne, his eyes burning like fire. I'd never seen such an expression on him before. Fearsome. Deadly. Secrets as ancient as the world itself protected beneath the impenetrable scales and horns on his skull. His voice was like a volcano about to erupt, turning my swaggering gate into a shuffle.

"COME CLOSER."

The gold pieces piled up were slipping like shale, and the entire cavern seemed to shake. I was thirty yards from the foot of his throne when I opened my mouth to speak; my day of glory had come.

"STOP!"

I froze. Something was wrong. Brenwar dropped to a knee beside me, head down.

My father sat there, monstrous claws clasped in his lap, a side of his razor sharp teeth bare.

"REMOVE YOUR ARMOR."

"With great joy, Father," I said, unstrapping the buckles on my chest plate. Certainly, he had to have noticed my dragon's hand at least, yet he said nothing. Perhaps, there was to be more of a ceremony with the full showing. I tossed my armor and garments aside, standing with my naked chest out, my incredible black scaled arm up high.

My father sucked his breath through his teeth, his face smoldering with fury, and roared so loud I thought the mountain had exploded.

I fell to the ground, holding my ears, crying out and pleading for mercy. I couldn't think or focus; I just screamed as I felt like the entire world was going to end. A sharp cracking sound exploded nearby as one of the marble columns fell. The room filled with heat so hot I could barely breathe. My whole world had gone wrong. I'd never been so terrified.

Somehow, I rose to my feet despite all the feeling in my legs being gone. My hands were still clamped over my ears as I watched my father continue his angry bellow. Brenwar was almost covered in treasure, his face devoid of expression, eyes watering like he'd seen a horrible ghost.

I yelled out, "What is wrong, Father?"

His roar stopped, but my ears kept on ringing.

His voice was lower now.

"What have you done?"

I stood, shaking, stupefied, and gawping.

"What have you done?" My father asked again, the rage in his voice gone, but the molten steel tone remaining. "Have you ever seen a black scaled dragon?"

I looked at my arm, shook my head, and said, "No."

Then, I realized something must be horribly wrong.

"The Ruffie you saved has been here and told me what you have done. I hoped that it was not true, though I knew that it was. Did you even realize that you killed so many?"

The truth was, I didn't have any idea how many I killed at all. I hadn't even thought about it.

My father looked down, and I felt like it was the last time I'd ever see him again. My heart began to sputter in my chest as I fell to my knees, tears streaming down my cheeks, and begged, "No, father, I'm so sorry. Let me fix this."

"It's too late for that. You have cursed yourself. You are no longer welcome in Dragon Home. You'll take no swords, no gold, no magic … not anything. You are on your own. If there is any hope left, you'll have to find it on your own. I've told you all I can. Now go, to never return unless those scales are a different color."

My father gave me one long lasting look with nothing but sadness and disappointment in his eyes. I'd failed him, I knew it, for the last time. I felt smaller than the tiniest coin in the room as he turned, walked away and disappeared back into the mural.

Alone, I wept my way through my father's throne room, never looking back, through Dragon Home, through the Sulfur Marsh, until I wept no more.

***

Bearded and lonely, I sat inside a cave at least a hundred leagues from my father, as another season passed while I contemplated my failure in self-pity. No men killed. No dragons saved. My cursed black scales remained.

If there is any hope left, you'll have to find it on your own, my father had said.

He'd said many things, and it was time I put them together. I rose from the crag where I had stooped and bellowed the fiercest bellow I could muster. It was time to figure out what I must do to become a dragon, a very good one, at that. Like my father.

From out of nowhere, Brenwar showed up and tossed a beautiful sword at my feet. It was Fang.

"Brenwar! How did you get this?" I asked in alarm and jubilation.

"Yer father only said *you* couldn't take anything from his cavern. He didn't say anything about me." He winked and added. "And that isn't all I got, either."

Thus begins the Chronicles of Dragon.

A note from the Author

The Hero, The Sword and The Dragons is my 8th published work and my 5th fantasy novel. I wanted to take moment to elaborate on where this new series is headed. This first introductory book is a novella (20,000 words), but future books will be twice as long (around 200 to 250 pages). My intent is to write a series of books appropriate for all ages but designed with younger (tweens), newer readers in mind. One of my goals is to encourage people to read, and I think lengthy and wordy books can be intimidating. I know when I was young I had trouble finding books that I could handle. Not every kid can dive into *Lord of the Rings*, but you can build up to that. So, I want to offer something that young readers will find exciting and easy to follow.

As for COD (The Chronicles of Dragon), the plan is for this to be a long running series, and I should turn out three or four 200-page books per year. Like my other fantasy series, *The Darkslayer*, these stories will be fast-paced and action-packed, but COD will be less, er, mature, and loaded with more magic and many, many dragons. Despite the PG-rated content, I think this series will still have something to offer for people of all ages. Thank you for reading this first book. I'm grateful.

Do good always,

Craig Halloran

About the Author

Craig Halloran resides with his family outside of his hometown, Charleston, West Virginia. When he isn't entertaining mankind, he is seeking adventure, working out, or watching sports. To learn more about him, go to: www.thedarkslayer.com

Other works by the author
The Darkslayer: Wrath of the Royals (Book 1)
The Darkslayer: Blades in the Night (Book 2)
The Darkslayer: Underling Revenge (Book 3)
The Darkslayer: Danger and the Druid (Book 4)
Zombie Day Care: Impact Series: Book 1
Zombie Rehab: Impact Series: Book 2
Jerk of All Trades: It's not him; it's them

In the works by the author
The Darkslayer (Book 5)
The Chronicles of Dragon: Dragon Bones and Tombstones (Book 2)

You can learn more about The Darkslayer and my other books at:
Facebook – The Darkslayer Report by Craig
Twitter – Craig Halloran

CPSIA information can be obtained at www.ICGtesting.com
Printed in the USA
LVOW07s1610150115

422984LV00009B/964/P